tanley T. Braverman opened a very important looking letter.

"Dear Stanley," it said. "Your aunt Fran lived to the age of 105. She left you all her possessions, but you will have to come and get them yourself."

So Stanley took the train all the way to Memphis and then walked until he reached a part of town where the houses leaned into the trees and the windows yawned in the sun. He knocked at number 45 Sneath Road. "Anybody there?" called Stanley.

When nobody answered, Stanley tiptoed in and went upstairs. In a room under the eaves, he discovered a wad of boy's clothes stuffed between the bed slats.

The pocket of a sailor suit still contained a stick of bubble gum. As the flavor swirled over Stanley's tongue, a forgotten summer flooded back as if sixty-five years was a wink on the smiling face of time.

THE SMALL WORLD OF
Binky Braverman

BY

ROSEMARY
WELLS

PICTURES BY

RICHARD
EGIELSKI

VIKING

T he evening of June 15, 1938, was as sticky as hot molasses when Binky Braverman came in for supper. Leech suckers plastered his legs. Poison ivy rashes crept up one bug-bitten arm and down the other. Rex, his collie, licked a dab of bait off Binky's ear.

"Stanley," said Binky's dad, "how would you like to spend the summer in the big city with Aunt Fran and Uncle Julius?"

"We're having a new baby," explained Binky's ma.

"But me and Archie and Kip are fixing to go back in the swamp at sunup," said Binky.

But it didn't matter what Binky said.

Uncle Julius and Aunt Fran met Binky's train at Union Station in Memphis, Tennessee.

"Stanley, you are so thin!" said Aunt Fran.

Binky was too afraid to tell them that his name was Binky.

"What's this in your hair?" Uncle Julius asked.

"Dried night crawlers," said Binky.

Aunt Fran cut them out with her nail scissors.

While Aunt Fran prepared dinner, Uncle Julius tuned into the *Royal Canadian Mounted Police Marching Band Hour* on the radio. He asked Binky if he liked school. Binky allowed that he hated it. Especially arithmetic.

Uncle Julius was an accountant. "Son," Uncle Julius whispered, "by August you'll never have a lick of trouble in school again! Why, you'll be able to take three million, multiply to the seventh power, and divide by twelve, all without pencil and paper."

Binky could not finish Aunt Fran's chicken paprika with noodle pudding. "We belong to the Clean Plate Club, Stanley!" said Aunt Fran.

At bath time, Aunt Fran scrubbed Binky squeaky with her Nila of the Nile bath products. She trimmed his nails as neat as a nurse.

Uncle Julius furnished him with Baritone Military Mouthwash. Both of them watched Binky brush his teeth.

Longing for Rex's warm muzzle in his ear, Binky fell into an uneasy sleep.

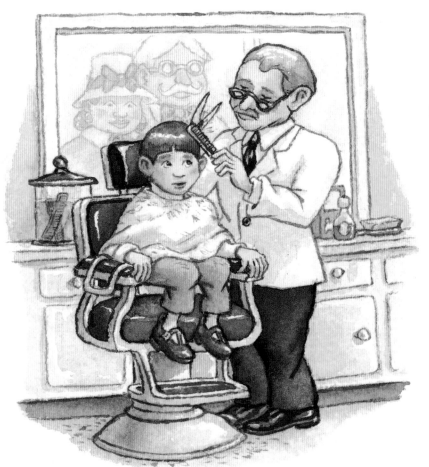

In the morning, Binky was taken
for a haircut.

Then it was off to the department store
for new clothes. Binky had never worn such
tight and itchy clothes.

After lunch, Binky was given a friend—the
dentist's boy, Leo. Leo only liked to play cards.

Because he cheated, Leo won
every game.

Somewhere in those summer evenings, red bugs whirred and frogs gulped, but in Aunt Fran and Uncle Julius's house, Jell-O salads and the Wonderful World of Fractions ruled the day.

Binky slept fretfully. In his dreams, numbers added themselves up wrong. Ketchup stains ruined shirt after shirt and Leo cheated him out of his membership in the Clean Plate Club.

One night in July after another math dream, Binky reached across the bed to pat Rex's furry flank. But Rex was not there. Archie and Kip were hundreds of miles away.

"I want to go home," Binky said. No one answered.

"I want to go home!" Binky said louder.

"Oh, stay with us," said a voice.

"Yes, stay!" several other voices chimed in. The voices seemed to be coming from the kitchen. Binky got out of bed and tiptoed downstairs.

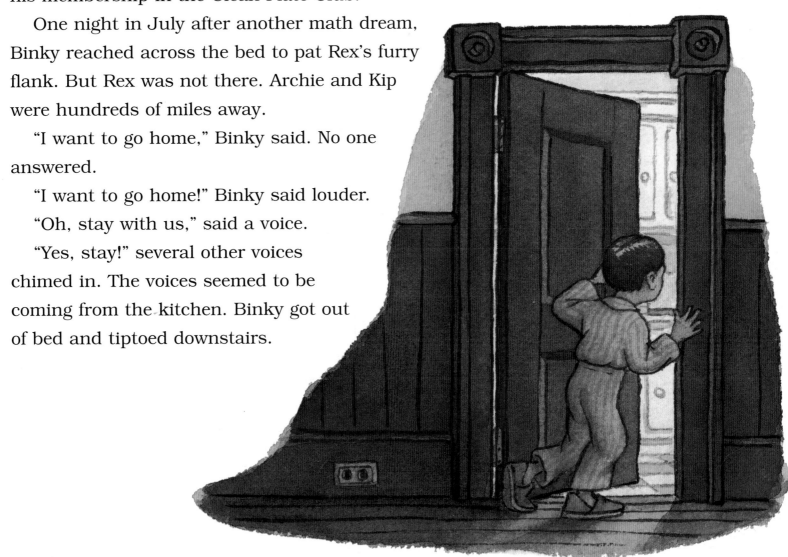

In the moonlight near the toaster stood a tiny musician. "Who are you?" asked Binky.

"I'm Sam, the Banjo Man," came the answer. "I just hopped off the kitchen matchbox. You've seen me there a hundred times next to the paprika!"

"But you're alive!" said Binky.

"Of course," said Sam. "We all are!"

The Paprika Twins jumped off the box of paprika and did the tango across the counter top.

"Wow!" said Binky.

From boxes and jars all over the kitchen hopped a crowd of inch-high folks. In the light of the stove clock they danced up a storm while Sam struck up "Mule Skinner's Saturday Night."

In the morning, Binky could not finish his waffles. The moment Aunt Fran turned her back, four Yellow Bears climbed off the syrup jug and gobbled up the waffles and half a sausage from Uncle Julius's plate.

"Thank you, Yellow Bears," whispered Binky.

"What was that?" asked Uncle Julius.

At eleven, Aunt Fran left for her beauty appointment. The early August air wafted through the open window, and Binky caught the scent of blackberries and sun-warmed mud. Before he knew what he was doing, Binky was eating fistfuls of berries and sliding down the clay hill into a hog wallow.

Later Binky moaned over his ruined clothes. "Mud sludge! Berry stains! Aunt Fran will never forgive me!"

"Don't worry, Binky," said a voice. "We'll take care of this lickety-split!"

On the laundry shelf was a box of Saint Joan Washing Powder. Saint Joan herself came to Binky's aid.

Joan was a leader. She shook the Bleach Bunny awake from his box and sat astride the iron like a motorcyclist. When Binky's clothes were good as new, Joan gave a piercing whistle.

"Your clothes are clean, but you're a mess," said Joan.

Nila of the Nile poured bubbles into a steamy tub while the Baritone belted out "The Peppermint Jingle."

Aunt Fran did not notice a thing.

After lunch, well on his way to losing a third game of rummy to Leo, Binky heard a sudden buzzing. A tiny propeller plane took off from the pack of Pilot playing cards and began circling the room.

The pilot's voice crackled over his radio. "Roger, do you read me? While he's shuffling the deck he's slipping the ace of spades down his shirt. Over and out!"

"Leo," Binky said, "I want to count the cards, please."

"Cockpit to base, do you read me?" came the pilot's voice. "He's dealing from the bottom of the deck! Make him stop! Over and out."

"Stop dealing from the bottom of the deck, Leo," said Binky.

The pilot's name was Ike. He divebombed Leo mercilessly.

Binky began to win. Leo went home in a snit.

At supper the Yellow Bears helped Binky with his shoo-fly pie. Aunt Fran didn't notice a thing. Nor did Uncle Julius detect any fluttering on the Blue Nun ink bottle as Binky twisted over his long division.

"Nothing better than a problem with nice big numbers," said the Blue Nun's cheery voice. In no time, six weeks of fractions were done correctly.

From that moment on, Binky was happy. Sam strummed for him. The Paprika Twins waltzed to "The Blue Danube." At night Ike landed his plane on Binky's pillow and told him stories of soaring above the mighty Mississippi in the starlight. Of all his new friends, Ike was the one Binky loved the best.

At last the news flashed that Binky had a baby sister. Tears filled Aunt Fran's and Uncle Julius's eyes. "We will miss you so much, Stanley," they said.

Before he left, Binky stuffed his new clothes under the slats of the bed. He packed his dear friends' boxes and bottles into his suitcase.

When he got home, Binky admired his baby sister for a couple of minutes. Then he went off in a leaky canoe with Archie, Kip, and Rex, to look for snapping turtles.

Later that night, Binky crept downstairs and unpacked his friends. No one moved from their boxes or bottles.

Binky shook the boxes. He called them by name. "Ike! Sam!" he shouted. "St. Joan! Nila!"

No one answered but the sap beetles, clicking away in the night wind.

"Ike, where are you? Oh, Ike, don't leave me!" Binky cried.

Rex licked Binky's face. With Ike's card box pressed beneath him, Binky drifted toward the land of dreams.

Suddenly a voice crackled, "Cockpit to base, cockpit to base, do you read me?"

"Ike!" Binky answered. "Ike, where are you?"

Through heavy static Ike's voice faded in and out. "We're heading out of range for now," he said, "but if in your true heart you are ever lonely again, why just set your sights on the blue horizon, get on the radio, and we'll read your signal loud and clear.

"Roger! Over and out!"

For Valerie —R.W.

For Uncle Billy —R.E.

VIKING

Published by Penguin Group

Penguin Young Readers Group, 345 Hudson Street, New York, New York 10014, U.S.A.

Penguin Books Ltd, 80 Strand, London WC2R 0RL, England

Penguin Books Australia Ltd, 250 Camberwell Road, Camberwell, Victoria 3124, Australia

Penguin Books Canada Ltd, 10 Alcorn Avenue, Toronto, Ontario, Canada M4V 3B2

Penguin Books (N.Z.) Ltd, 182-190 Wairau Road, Auckland 10, New Zealand

First published in 2003 by Viking, a division of Penguin Young Readers Group

1 3 5 7 9 10 8 6 4 2

LIBRARY OF CONGRESS CATALOGING-IN-PUBLICATION DATA

Wells, Rosemary.

The small world of Binky Braverman / by Rosemary Wells ; illustrated by Richard Egielski.

p. cm.

Summary: Binky Braverman's stay with his aunt and uncle in Memphis unexpectedly proves to be full of adventure when characters
on the boxes and jars in their kitchen come to life and become his friends.

ISBN 0-670-03636-6 (hardcover)

[1. Loneliness—Fiction. 2. Imagination—Fiction. 3. Aunts—Fiction. 4.Uncles—Fiction.
5. Memphis (Tenn.)—Fiction.] I. Egielski, Richard, ill. II. Title.

PZ7.W46843Sm 2003   [E]—dc21   2003002407

Printed in the U.S.A.

Set in Bookman